All Books by Harper Lin

www.HarperLin.com

Death of a Snowman

An Emma Wild Mystery
Book #3

by Harper Lin

Contents

Chapter 1

The children were gone. Almost without a trace, if it hadn't been for the hand-written note dangling from one of the "hands" of the snowman to inform us that they had indeed been taken. At least I heard rumors of this note – a ransom note probably – that the police had removed before the crowd gathered.

The town square was a media circus. The townspeople should've been at home eating their dinners, but curiosity got the best of them and they gathered at the scene of the crime to see the newly infamous snowman. It had been made by the abducted children, mayor Richard Champ's daughter Zoe, six, and son Joseph, four, for the contest.

Even though the snowman section of the town square was sectioned off by police tape, everyone stood around and snapped pictures of this sinister looking snowman. Its carrot nose had been taken from its rightful spot on the face and inserted into one of the branch "hands". The branch had been repositioned at a higher angle, holding the carrot in such a way that it looked like a knife, ready to stab at whoever got in its way.

The other "hand" had held the note, which had disappeared into the hands of the police.

"How dreadful," said an old lady in the crowd to her friend. "Those poor children."

"What kind of monster would do this?" her friend exclaimed. "And to make a joke out of it?"

"A sick, twisted game." A man in his fifties shook his head at no one in particular.

The snowman did look menacing with its squinty pebble eyes, hollow nose and cruel snarl. I zoned in on it with my camera phone and snapped a few pictures. The whole thing intrigued me. I had to help the case in any way that I could, especially now that I was friends with the mayor's wife, Eleanor.

All around me, the townspeople of Hartfield muttered their grievances with the kidnapping and the distasteful way the kidnapper flaunted it in our faces. It was such a big ordeal that reporters and news crews came all the way from Toronto to report it.

My very pregnant sister, Mirabelle, put her arm around me and squeezed my shoulder with reassurance.

"Who knew this town could be so dangerous?" she said. "Child abductors now?"

She stroked her belly to soothe herself. There had been a couple of murders in Hartfield recently, but when children were involved in a crime, it was beyond fear and anger. There was outrage.

The crowd was shushed by a news crew producer. The camera turned on, the light flashing in the attractive brunette reporter's freshly made up face. I pulled my coat hood up to stay incognito within the crowd in case the camera panned my way.

"Police are still on a wild goose chase to find the mayor's two missing children in Hartfield, Ontario. They went missing in the middle of the Snowman Festival earlier this afternoon, here in the town square at Hartfield. The children were taken after they had completed their snowman for the Snowman Building Competition. Police are questioning everyone in connection with the children and the festival contest. If you have information, please contact the police. A ransom note had been left in the hands of the snowman, threatening the lives of the children, although police will not be releasing the official contents of the note as of this moment..."

Up until the kidnapping, Hartfield had been a fun place for me to be, even though the holidays were over. The locals and tourists alike looked forward to the Annual Snowman Festival that took place every January. It was something that started twenty-five years ago to cure the winter blues. The time between New Year's Day and Valentine's Day was usually boring, if not depressing, in the cold weather and the festival was a way to get people excited again.

I had been looking forward to the festival too, since I'd missed the last five Snowman Festivals due to work. It was always something I used to enjoy as a child. There were contests, performances, plenty of food, and free stuff given out by people dressed up like snowmen.

I used to enter the snowman-building contest with Mirabelle all the time, and once we even won second prize, which was a fancy four-slice toaster that my father thoroughly appreciated.

It was nice to be back in the town where I grew up. When I was eighteen, I set off for New York to be a singer. After a few years of singing at open mics, my career finally took off. Now, I was what you would consider to be a celebrity, although I still felt a little strange about it sometimes. For the most part, I was used to the paparazzi, adoring fans, and nosy journalists. It was all part of the game. What was real to me was my family and my little Canadian hometown.

My third album was about to be released on Valentine's Day, and I had been AWOL from the usual promotional stuff, even though my manager, Rod, the guy who had discovered me, was calling me up and bugging me like crazy now that he had finally gotten over his holiday haze of binge drinking and general gluttony.

I wanted to take a break from the industry, but taking this long of a break wasn't my style. I was usually quite the workaholic, touring and promoting all the time, but getting by unnoticed in Hartfield had been a nice change.

However, over a week ago, the mayor found out who I was and that I was in town. I had been in Hartfield since December, but I supposed he didn't know who I was and wouldn't have cared if it wasn't for the fact that his wife, Eleanor, was a big fan of my music. She suggested the idea of making January 18th Emma Wild Day in Hartfield. This was certainly wild. Sure, winning Grammys and topping the album charts were accomplishments, but getting my own *day*? This was something else.

The funny thing was that most people in town didn't have a clue who I was – mainly because half the population was over the age of fifty – but Eleanor explained that Emma Wild Day would attract more tourists, which would boost the town's economy. I loved this town and I wanted to help in any way that I could, so how could I have said no?

The inauguration of Emma Wild Day took place a few days before the Snowman Festival. It wasn't a huge celebration. I just went on the stage to receive a plaque, shook hands with the mayor and posed for photo ops. He made a lovely speech about my career and how much I had contributed to the music industry. I was sure that Eleanor wrote most of the speech for him, but it was still rather touching.

Only local reporters knew about the surprise event and who broke the news before the major outlets did, so the paparazzi didn't have time to descend. I told the reporters the lie that I would be traveling to promote my third album soon so that media types wouldn't come and harass me in town after the fact.

So it had been a quiet but lovely affair. My family members were in the audience, as well as a group of about a hundred fans I didn't know I had in town. I signed autographs and there were plenty of coffee and snacks for everyone, catered by my sister's Chocoholic Cafe. My fans here weren't as zealous or crazy as the fans in New York or the ones I met backstage at my concerts. Hartfield was a quiet Canadian town, and Canadians were too cool to care much about most things.

I was relieved because I was used to being photographed whenever I stepped out of my apartment in Manhattan, but here, I got to chat with fans about the most random things. I probably spent about half an hour talking to one lady about scrapbooking. It was just that kind of town.

The only glitch in the day was when I spotted Sterling Matthews lurking somewhere in the crowd. Usually I would've been happy to see him, but he was with someone else – a pretty brunette with a ponytail and wearing a burnt orange jacket. It wasn't his ex-wife because I'd seen photos of her and she was blonde.

Was Sterling on a date? He only passed through the crowd with her, avoiding my direction and any kind of acknowledgement.

But that was supposed to be the deal. Sterling had agreed that he wouldn't contact me for the month until I made up my mind between him and my ex Nick Doyle.

Nick was in Morocco reshooting scenes for an action movie and I hadn't heard from him either. I did see a picture of him in the papers recently. He was laughing with his cute female co-star. Rumors were spreading like wildfire about the heat and chemistry between the two of them, but I tried not to give them a second thought. Rumors were rumors. He'd been linked to every woman he'd starred in a movie with, and I'd been linked to every bachelor – and a couple of married men – I was photographed standing next to, so I knew that it was all a bunch of baloney.

I hoped.

Still, between Nick's rumored new love and Sterling's apparent date, there was the chance that I didn't have to decide anymore. Maybe they'd both moved on.

As hurt as I was, I couldn't blame them entirely. It probably didn't feel too great when the one you loved couldn't decide between you and another man. Maybe I had expected too much for them to be understanding.

The thing was, I had come to a decision about who I wanted to be with only a week after Nick left for Morocco. It took a while for me to get used to the idea and accept the decision. Now I wondered if it was too late.

On the bright side, taking the time to be alone in the past month gave me the chance to assess my career – and my life. I wrote a bunch of new songs. They were much happier, optimistic songs. Some of them weren't even about heartbreak or romantic love, which was a huge departure for me, since I was that singer who always crooned about being unlucky in love.

I was done with singing depressing songs. They were still nice songs and people really liked them, but I didn't want the songs to translate into my real life anymore. I wrote new songs about the love of family, of friends, of life in general. I took it as a sign that I was heading into a better phase in my life as I headed into my thirties. No longer would I depend on a man for my happiness and self-esteem. I had the strength to create my own happiness as long as I was surrounded by loving, supportive people. A relationship was only the icing on top of a rich, delicious cake.

After celebrating Emma Wild Day, I felt utterly ready to take on the world again. No more hiding out from the press or even people in town. I vowed to do more charity work this year and give back rather than fret over my love life. I wanted to meet new people, take on new projects and develop deeper relationships with my fans.

Things had been going well until the kidnapping happened. The children had probably been taken when I was on stage singing at the Snowman Festival. It had been a surprise performance with only three songs in my set.

The festival was a popular event. I had kept an eye on the snowman building contest because that was my favorite activity. All the built snowmen were behind my little audience, so it was just close enough that I could make out the outlines of the people who were busy building, but too far to see who they were exactly.

I had already met little Zoe and Joseph on Emma Wild Day. They were absolutely adorable children, so when I saw them building their snowman, I glanced back at them a few times. By the end of my set however, I thought I saw them talking to someone: a man, too thin to be the mayor. Then the man left and they continued on building the snowman.

After my set was over, I changed into my normal clothes and walked around the festival. I checked out all the snowmen that the contestants had built – the children were nowhere to be seen. I had thought this was because they had finished their snowman early and Eleanor had taken them to get ice cream or something before the judging began. At the time, their snowman hadn't had its nose repositioned nor had a ransom note tied to one "hand."

That would happen later, after Eleanor became frantic because the children were nowhere to be found when the festival was over.

I wondered who this man was, the man who had been talking to the children. It was as if he knew them. And was I the only one who had seen him?

Chapter 2

I tried calling Sterling right after we found out that the mayor's children had been kidnapped, but his phone was off. He must've been busy working on the case. I wanted to tell him about what I had seen from the stage, even if it wasn't much to go on. I left a couple of messages saying that I wanted to meet, but I fell asleep before he called back and left a message saying that he would be working all night.

I wanted to visit Sterling at the office first thing in the morning. As I walked out the door, Rod, my manager, called. I sighed, but I answered it anyway. At least it was something to do as I walked to the station, and I had been avoiding his calls for the past couple of days.

"Well, well, well," he said. "I thought you were dead."

"Is that why they have a day named after me now?" I joked.

"You're very impressed with yourself these days, aren't you?"

"Aren't I always?"

"Are you really still stuck in that little nowhere town?" Rod yawned.

He was one of the coolest managers around, having been a rock star himself in his twenties. He quit around my age though, claiming that he did so in order to save his own life. Any more of the rock and roll lifestyle and he would've been dead face down in a toilet bowl. Knowing how he lived now at the age of fifty-eight, I believed him.

"Yes," I replied. "Things were pretty calm around here until these children got kidnapped."

"Children, yeah, what a shame." Rod yawned again, not sounding the least bit interested. He was a New Yorker, after all. "Tell me, what's the deal with this Snowman Festival anyway?"

"What do you mean?"

"What's there to celebrate? Is Santa Claus, Cupid and the Easter Bunny not enough for you people?"

I chuckled. "Well, it's based on this Hartfield legend. Our founder, Henry Hartfield was said to have been guided to this town by a snowman after he wandered off from a group of explorers."

"What? You mean he met a man covered in snow?"

"No. A real snowman, a man made completely out of snow. I know it sounds ridiculous, but that's how the story goes. It was over a hundred years ago, and Henry Hartfield was rumored to be addicted to opium, so it's probably a bunch of crap."

Rod exploded into laughter. "Of all the ridiculous stories I've heard in the world, I have to live until I have one foot in the grave to hear about a town founded by a magical snowman?"

"This is why I don't go around telling people this story," I said. "January twenty-first is Henry Hartfield's birthday, but it has always been Snowman Day by default. Kind of like Santa overshadowing Jesus."

"Or the Easter bunny overshadowing Jesus, again. That Jesus can't get a break."

Rod kept laughing until I could practically hear the tears dripping from his eyes.

"All right, all right, I know you called me for something other than a ridiculous history lesson."

When the laughing subsided, Rod got down to business. "All the talk shows are calling. So are the journalists. You did the cover shoot for *Rolling Stone* ages ago but you still haven't confirmed for the interview. The magazine's out in February for God's sake. Work with me here."

"I'm sorry," I said. "I've been taking some personal weeks; you know that."

"Months is more like it. Your record company's getting annoyed. They're questioning if you're doing your promotional duties. It's not looking good. Oh, and *New Woman* called. They want you on the cover."

"Really?" I wrinkled my nose. I wasn't thrilled about the idea of being on a cover with my tiny boobs pushed all the way to my neck with two pushup bras, and being surrounded by headlines with references to sex and vaginas. Once was enough.

"I know," said Rod. "I told them no, that you're all booked up. Which you are. You have two talk show appearances next week."

"What? I do?"

"Yes, I told you ages ago. Now, you're booked for a flight to LAX on —"

"I can't!" I said. "It's crazy here. As I told you, these children are kidnapped and I have to help solve the case."

"But, honey, they have detectives for that."

"I know, but I can help —"

"Darling, you're more Nancy Sinatra than Nancy Drew. You have a job to fulfill, responsibilities, and my ass on the line."

"I know, but hopefully I'll crack the case in a couple of days. I think I only have a couple days anyway before the children are murdered so it's not like I have a choice."

"Murdered? That's tacky."

"Rod? I have to go now. I'm at the station."

"Emma —"

I hung up. I had been in a rush earlier to get to the station, but now that I was there, I hesitated.

What if Sterling didn't want to see me? And did I want to see him? I'd had no contact with Sterling or Nick for over three weeks now, and to tell you the truth, it had been peaceful. I spent all my time with my parents, with Mirabelle, and a couple of girlfriends. We had a few girls' nights and even a sleepover once and it felt like old times. But I had to face the music sometime; there was no avoiding Sterling. I had to tell him about what I saw on stage. I took a deep breath and pushed the doors open.

Chapter 3

Ever since Emma Wild Day, some of the guys at the police station were aware of who I was now. Before I was just the crazy chick that was always following Sterling around on cases.

However, Sterling would never talk about his love life to his colleagues. He was just that private.

When I came in, the guys greeted me with more enthusiasm than I'd received in the past. I flashed them a smile and told them I was here to see Sterling. Some of their eyes lingered on me, even though I was in a puffy winter coat. I did make an effort with hair and makeup that day. I hadn't officially seen Sterling for three weeks, after all.

His office door was wide open, but before I went in, I peeked through his office's big glass window. Sterling looked like he hadn't slept all night. He had dark circles under his eyes and a thick five o'clock shadow that made him look more rugged than ever. His dark hair was perfectly messed up and the light of his grey eyes had dimmed from their usual brightness.

I poked my head in the door. "Hey."

He looked up, slightly startled by the sight of me.

"Emma, hi. What are you doing here?"

Smiling seemed to take all his energy, but he smiled nonetheless. In his stressed out state, I appreciated the effort.

"How's it going with the case?" I asked eagerly.

"It's been hectic," he said.

"What have you done so far?"

"I've been talking to the mayor's family to get leads."

I sat down on the chair across from his desk. "So what have you found? Have you received further communication from the kidnapper?"

"No." Sterling looked deflated. "Nothing. Oh, and congratulations on Emma Wild Day. I wanted to call you, but, you know."

His voice trailed off. I wished it were the right moment to tell him that I wanted to be with him, but we were in the middle of a kidnapping case. It wasn't exactly a romantic moment to break the news. Plus, maybe he was dating someone else. It wasn't the right time to have this conversation yet.

"Did you find any leads?" I asked.

"The mayor does have a few enemies. Political competitors for this year's election for example. And it took hours for Champ to admit this, but a few years before he was elected, he took part in a money laundering scheme that had been unsuccessful. Now he thinks that the same guys he was in business with are out to get him."

"Wow," I said. "So you're tracking all these leads?"

"Yup. My new partner's out questioning Stewart Branson, the mayor's biggest competition for reelection, and I'm about to head out to tail one of the money laundering guys."

"What about the mayor's wife?" I asked. "She could have enemies too."

"We already thought of that." A female voice came from behind me.

I turned around in my chair. It was the brunette I saw with Sterling on Emma Wild Day.

"I'm Detective Sandra Palmer." She stepped into the room. "Sterling's new partner."

I took her outstretched hand and shook it.

"Emma Wild, nice to meet you."

She gave me a quick once-over, and I thought I detected a sneer.

"So you're our local celebrity."

Even though I was used to being judged and criticized by the public, I still felt self-conscious from time to time and this was one of those times. I was wearing a white cashmere sweater and cream-colored pants. With makeup on and hair in waves that could only come from a curling iron, I felt extra girly.

In contrast, Sandra was a barefaced beauty wearing a dark pantsuit. Sterling might not have gotten much sleep, but Sandra looked refreshed. She had her dark brown hair tied back into a neat bun. With her big brown eyes, olive skin, and the fullest lips I'd ever seen, she was definitely pretty. Gorgeous, in fact. Although she was in a boring pantsuit, I could tell that she had a good figure.

My heart sank. I met beautiful women all the time, but not one to work 24/7 with Sterling.

"I didn't know Sterling had a new partner," I said. "What happened to Philip?"

Sterling cleared his throat. Was he nervous?

"He got engaged and relocated to Ottawa, where his fiancée lives."

"Yes," Sandra answered. "I heard about this opening from Toronto and I applied and got it through recommendations from my superiors. I always wanted to be a detective, so I didn't mind moving to a small town if I could fast-track and become one. So here I am."

"Great." I smiled. "Congratulations. How is the case going?"

"I'm sorry, but the information is confidential. I know that you're Sterling's friend, but it's classified."

"I see," I said slowly, "but I wanted to help. Actually I have some information to give you."

Sandra raised an eyebrow. "Oh? Sure, whatever info you have would help if you know anything."

"Well, first of all, I thought that Edward Herman, the dairy farmer, could be a suspect. Sterling and I discovered that he was, well, *connected* with the mayor's wife."

"I know the story," Sandra said, sounding unimpressed. "Sterling told me about your little run-in with Edward and how he was having an affair with Eleanor Champ."

She let out an amused laugh.

"We got one of our boys on him, in fact," Sterling added quickly.

"Yes," said Sandra. "Thanks, Emma, but we've got it covered. Edward seems to be going about his daily routine, and our guy has nothing to report other than the fact that he'd been calling Eleanor Champ at least two times a day to check in on her, so I think he's off the list. Anybody else that you suspect?"

Her constantly arching eyebrow was beginning to annoy me. It was like a question mark to challenge answers out of me that she knew I didn't have. Plus she looked at me like I was some sort of bimbo.

"I did see the children when I was performing on stage," I said, mustering as much confidence and certainly as I could. I set up the scene for them, of how far they were and what I noticed. "I saw a man talk to them."

Sterling frowned. "Who?"

"Well, I couldn't tell since they were so far, but I remember looking at him, wondering if he was the mayor, but quickly decided he wasn't because he was thinner."

"What color hair did he have?" Sandra asked. "How tall was he?"

"I'm sorry. They were so far away that I couldn't distinguish any features."

"So is there anything more you can tell us about him then?" asked Sandra.

"All I know was that a man talked to them. I saw them while I was singing, so I wasn't paying complete attention. The next time I glanced their way, the children were gone and it was the end of my set."

"But it could've been anybody," said Sandra. "Our team is interviewing all the witnesses they can find. If they saw someone, they would surely let us know. I mean, there were plenty of people at the festival."

"That's the thing," I said. "I think if he was a stranger, wouldn't somebody notice him? What if the guy was someone the children already know? Maybe he's a friend of the family."

"Are you sure that the person was even a man?" Sandra's eyebrow arched again.

I thought about it. "Whoever it was had short hair, so it's a possibility that it could be a woman, yes."

"It's really very little to go on," Sandra said. "It could've been anybody. Maybe just a friendly neighbour or something. You didn't actually see the man take the children, right?"

I hated to admit it, but Sandra was right. Maybe it was nothing.

"I just thought you might want to know this bit of info," I said. "It seemed strange that the children would be gone just moments after the man left."

"Well, thanks for taking the time." Sandra smiled condescendingly. "We'll continue to interview people at the festival and see if anyone else has a more detailed description of this man."

She stared at me, as if waiting for me to go. My gaze reverted to Sterling, who said nothing and only put on a strained smile in the midst of the tension.

My eyes fell to a ziplock bag on the table. There was a piece of paper inside.

"Is that the ransom note?"

Before they could answer, I jumped up to read it. It was written in a funny cursive writing, sloppy, like a child's.

"The twisted sunlight of morning's path; to the land of turmoil in the night's dead; children's laughter echoes hollow..."

"Please!" Sandra's pretty face twisted into a less pretty scowl. "This is classified information."

She grabbed the note from the desk.

"I'm good at solving cases," I said. "Let me help."

Sterling spoke up for me. "Yes, Emma has a knack for this. She can be an asset."

Sandra shot him a look. "This is against police regulations. You can have your badge suspended for divulging information to the public. We have plenty of boys on the case, and Sterling and I have plenty of experience. Let us professionals handle it."

"I just have this hunch that the kidnapper is close to the family. Whoever he is probably knows the children —"

Sandra raised an arm and cut me off. "Now of course this kidnapper knows who the children are. They're famous. Maybe celebrities don't have the perspective that we civilians do. The mayor's family is in the public eye. Everybody knows who they are." She sighed impatiently. "Celebrity or not, you can't just waltz into our office and start pointing fingers. We have a system in place and we are working as hard as we can. We have no time to waste on the silly musings of an outsider."

I looked at Sterling, but he looked defeated. He didn't defend me again.

Sandra's arm pointed to the door and I went out.

I turned around and tried one more time, "I just think —"

The door slammed in my face.

Chapter 4

The nerve of that woman. I stormed out of the station, absolutely livid, and headed straight to Mirabelle's cafe.

The lineup for coffee and chocolate wasn't as long as it usually was, and Mirabelle was behind the counter helping another barista make the drinks. When I came in, she saw how upset I was and waved me back to her office. We were sisters; we could communicate without speaking.

I plopped down on her blue beanie chair at the corner of her office and told her all that had transpired at the station with Sterling and Sandra.

"She sounds so rude," Mirabelle exclaimed. "Slamming a door in your face. I know they're under a lot of stress, but that's uncalled for."

She got up and took out a box from her freezer. After fumbling around back there, she slid me a red velvet cupcake on a plate with a plastic fork.

"This is absolute amazing. You have to try this."

"Thanks Mirabelle," I said.

I dug into the cupcake, straight for the centre. The cheesecake filling oozed out. I shoved half of the thing in my mouth and felt better immediately. It would've been better if it was warm, but you couldn't go wrong with a red velvet cupcake.

"Don't let her get to you," she said. "Maybe it's not personal. She might be the high-strung type."

But I couldn't help thinking that Sterling and Sandra looked like they would make a good couple. They were both detectives and gorgeous. Sandra was the smart type. I had always been terrible at school. I never studied and only thrived in music class and art class.

What had I been thinking when I wanted to follow Sterling to college at eighteen? No wonder he wanted to break up with me then. He knew I wasn't the smart type. They probably had plenty more in common. Plus they'd be working together all the time and who knew what would happen when they spent a lot of time together.

When I expressed all this to Mirabelle she gave me a quizzical look.

"That's funny," she said dryly. "I can't believe you're actually jealous. You're one of the most popular singers right now. Your face is on more covers of magazines than mine is in the picture frames at my house. Men are practically drooling over you. Not to mention there are two very hot men fighting over you right now, and one happens to be the hottest movie star of our time. Plus you're gorgeous. Don't you know that?"

I shook my head. "That's just makeup. And some designer clothes and a gay hairdresser who's really good with a hairbrush."

"You're just crazy." Mirabelle shook her head. "You write your own songs and your albums have sold millions. For God's sake, no wonder the lady detective slammed the door in your face. Now that I think about it, I'd slam a door in your face too."

That didn't cheer me up. I was still sullen, even with the cupcake all gone.

"When you were with Nick, he was probably working morning to night with hot actresses, right?"

"Right," I mumbled.

"And he didn't cheat on you. He wants to marry you."

"You're right." I nodded, trying to convince myself. "It's just a bunch of silly fears. But...she wore a pantsuit, and has a badge and a gun and everything."

"So?"

"She's a real detective," I said. "I'm just some silly wannabe. I don't even know how to use a gun."

"Look, you solved, what, two murder cases now? You're intuitive and have a knack for this kind of thing. Intuition can come in handy more than logic sometimes, right?"

"I suppose," I said. "I just want to help on this case, but she's shutting me out. I guess she's just being professional."

"If you can't work with Sterling, why not do it on your own? You're wasting time stuffing yourself with my baked goods, even if they are the best in town."

"Why are you always right?" I sighed and smiled. Mirabelle's pep talk and a cupcake did wonders for my spirit. "Those kids have to be found. I hope they're all right. I met them, and they're lovely. Sterling and Sandra might be going in one direction, but they don't have everyone covered." I thought about the case a bit more. "It could be someone closer than they think. Once I read about this kidnapping case in Connecticut where a little boy got kidnapped. It turned out that it was the gardener who was fired over some dead geraniums and he wanted to get revenge on the parents."

"And what happened?" asked Mirabelle. "Was the boy okay?"

"Unfortunately he locked the boy in a car trunk for too long. Since it was a particularly hot summer, the trunk was overheated and the boy died."

"Wow. I hope the guy got what he deserved."

"Two life sentences," I said. "The thing is, I'm not sure if this kidnapping is about money. The ransom note didn't say anything about money. It was just sort of...cruel."

I told Mirabelle what the note said. The handwriting on the note was scrawled by someone who wanted to disguise his or her writing. It looked like it had been written with the left hand so that it would be hard to analyze.

"I wonder what the motive is," Mirabelle said. "It does sounds like someone wants to torture the parents."

"Exactly," I said. "Whoever this is wants the mayor or his wife to suffer. Or both, but who would go out of their way to be this cruel? The dairy farmer is out. Plus, when I did speak to him, it sounded like he genuinely cared for Eleanor, so I don't think he would do this to her, even if he wanted to get back at the mayor."

"I don't even think the mayor's all that rich," said Mirabelle. "He's only a small town mayor. He may live in a better house now, but he used to live in a house the same as ours a few years ago."

"Right, which is why I do think this crime is more personal. But who would really want to hurt him? It could be the money-laundering people, I suppose. But if it's them, Sterling's team would surely dig up something. But I can't ask him because I don't want to get him in trouble."

"Is it him?" Mirabelle asked softly. "Did you choose Sterling?"

I hesitated to answer, but I was dying to tell someone. "Yes. I thought about it long and hard. I choose Sterling."

Mirabelle grinned. "I knew it."

"He was always the one who got away. I do love Nick, I really do. Heck, once I was madly obsessed with him. But my life wasn't going in the direction I wanted with him. I'm not sure that he would cut back on the work and travel if we did marry. He's just too in demand. What if he falls back into his old patterns? Meanwhile, Sterling's always been a rock. I need that kind of security right now."

"It's hard to forget your first love." Mirabelle nodded in sympathy.

"Right. I've always wondered, 'what if?'"

I looked at Mirabelle's huge baby bump.

"I mean, I'm not sure if I'm quite ready for kids yet, but I'd like the option. Soon."

"I hear you," said Mirabelle. "But sometimes I envy you and your life. You get to travel around, meet all these interesting people. And what do I get to do?"

"Eat chocolate and drink coffee all day," I teased. "What torture."

"So you want to quit your celebrity lifestyle and come back here?"

"No. I can't stop singing. I'll just have to slow down my career. I've already accomplished what I wanted. I'll just have to keep challenging myself musically. But I can do that here too. I can buy a house and build my own studio. Why not? Sure, I'll have to tour and promote, but that's only sometimes. It's not going to kill me if I appear on fewer covers of magazines."

"But what if Nick wants that too? Buying a house and settling down with you?"

"He said he wants his career to slow down," I said. "But I don't know. I feel like Sterling is a more sensible choice."

"Which one is better in bed?" Mirabelle smiled slyly.

"Mirabelle!" I exclaimed. "I'm not going to talk about that with you."

Chapter 5

Once I picked myself up from my moment of self-pity, I decided to pay Eleanor Champ a visit at her house. If Sandra didn't want me on the case, I would go around her. It wasn't hard to arrange a meeting to see Eleanor because she was a big fan of mine. We had talked quite a bit after the Emma Wild Day ceremony, and we got along really well.

I took a taxi to the Champ estate. The house-keeper opened the door. She was a short stout lady wearing a grey apron that matched her knotty hair. When she saw me, she narrowed her eyes, all the wrinkles crinkling on her face like a road map.

"I'm here to see Mrs. Champ?"

"Who's inquiring?" she asked sharply.

"Emma Wild," I said. "I'm a friend."

"Stay here." She closed the door in my face.

What was with all the doors slamming in my face today? It reminded me of the early days of my career when I used to visit record companies with my demo.

I heard her taking her sweet time trudging up the stairs while I waited outside in the winter cold. By the time I began to worry whether I was getting frostbite, the door opened, and the sour house-keeper appeared once again.

"She's upstairs," she barked. "First room to your left."

"Okay," I said. "Thanks."

I walked up quickly, eager to get away from her.

Eleanor was sitting in a library room looking perfectly composed and beautiful. She wore a baby blue sweater, a knee-length corduroy skirt and tan leather boots. With her immaculate ivory skin and blonde hair, she looked very well kept for someone in her early fifties. All the walls were lined with books. Sunlight streamed from the window, lighting her from behind and giving her a golden aura. She was drinking her tea when she saw me, and had I not known better I would've thought that she was just enjoying a quiet morning to herself.

"Ah, Emma."

She stood up to greet me, but I signalled that it was okay for her to sit. I closed the door behind me, and sat in the chair next to her.

"Would you like some tea?" She gestured the empty cup and saucer on the tea tray next to the pot.

Her lips were smiling, but her eyes weren't. They were red, probably from hours of crying last night and this morning.

"I'll help myself," I said. "How are you holding up?"

For a second, Eleanor couldn't speak. Then I noticed her lower lip quivering before she pressed her lips together. She was trying not to cry.

"I trust the police are doing all they can," she finally said.

"Yes," I agreed.

I sure hoped Sterling and his new partner were getting somewhere.

"I just don't know what this person would want," she said. "They're not asking for money. Yet."

She teared up and sobbed. I stood up and put my arm around her shoulders.

"They'll turn up," I said, trying to sound convincing.

"I'm such a bad mother," she said. "Maybe this is God punishing me."

"That's not true. I've seen you with your kids and you're a great mother. Those kids love you."

She continued to sob and I passed her a napkin from the tea tray.

"Whoever took them is out to get me for all that I've done. I'm a terrible wife and a terrible mother."

I didn't know whether to bring it up, but now it felt appropriate.

"Eleanor, you can't torture yourself like this. I know about your...affair."

Her blue eyes grew wide. "You know?"

I nodded. "With Edward Herman, the dairy farmer, yes."

She buried her face in the napkin and made a sound that was between a laugh and a cry.

"How humiliating," she said. "Does the whole town know?"

"No. Not at all. I only know because I was questioning him for a murder case. Remember the woman who owned the inn? Edward used to date her."

"Oh. And you suspected him of murder. I remember the police calling me about his alibi. So you were with the detective?"

"Yes. I helped with the case."

"That's impressive," she said.

"Thanks. Well, I wanted to help you with this case too. I know that the police are doing all they can to go after all the leads in connection with the mayor – where is Richard anyway?"

"I'm not sure," she said. "He might've gone to his office to work."

"Does Richard know about Edward?" I asked.

"I don't know. If he did, he probably wouldn't even care. He probably has his own mistress, or two. I wouldn't know or care either. All he really cares about is his political career. Wants to move to Toronto and be the mayor there in the near future."

"Is that something you want to do?"

"I thought I did. Before I met Edward." Her voice got quiet. "I wish Edward were here."

"Why don't you just get a divorce?"

"And have two failed marriages?" She let out a bitter laugh.

Looking at Eleanor in that pristine room, in that big fancy house with servants, I supposed she was the type to keep up appearances.

"But you do love Edward?"

"Yes," she said. "Even if he is a dairy farmer. But I wanted to wait until the kids are grown to leave Richard. Richard and I have a good understanding anyhow."

"How is Richard with the children?"

Eleanor turned pink, or was it just my imagination?

"He loves them, of course. He's worried to bits."

"Does he know who would take them?"

"He does suspect some of the men he used to be in business with, so I'm praying that they catch them soon."

"But do you think it might be somebody else?" I watched her carefully.

Eleanor sighed. "I don't know. I wish I did. All I know is that I've sinned and I'm being punished. I just hope that God doesn't take it out on the children. The thing is, at the festival, I left them. It was my fault. I left the kids on their own while I stood by Richard's side to work the festival and greet the visitors."

She began to sob loudly.

"Oh, Eleanor, it's not your fault. It was planned. There was a note, so this person was waiting for a chance to take them."

"But who? And why would the kids go so easily?"

"That's why I suspect that it might be someone your family is close to."

Her teary eyes grew wide again. "You think?"

"It's what I'm trying to figure out," I said. "How many people are working or living in this house?"

"Well, there's me, Richard, Joseph and Zoe, our housekeepers Joanne and her husband Henry. They cook and Henry also tends to the garden."

"That's everyone?" I asked. "Are there people who come here often?

"Sometimes my eldest son Matthew comes to stay," she said. "He's eighteen and going to Callen University, so he usually lives on campus. There's also our babysitter Isla, who works part-time."

"I see."

"Do you really suspect someone in this house? I just can't imagine any one of them being involved in this!"

"I wouldn't rule it out," I said.

"But I trust them," Eleanor said.

"All of them?"

"Why, yes. Joanne and Henry like the kids. Joanne was taking care of the kids for a while, but she had back trouble so we hired Isla. She's been working with us for a couple of years, and she's great with them. There's no reason why any of them would want to kidnap my poor Joseph and Zoe."

"I'm not accusing anyone," I said. "I just want to know all the facts. Be aware of your surroundings is what my bodyguard always tells me. It could be someone in connection with the people who work for you as well. We just don't know so we have to be careful."

Eleanor took a deep breath. "Okay."

"Please tell me about the babysitter."

"Isla? I found her through a nanny agency. She had good recommendations from the previous families she'd worked for."

"So she doesn't live here," I asked.

"No. She picks the kids up from school and takes them home, feeds them and plays with them. She's studying literature at the same university as Matthew actually."

"Oh, are they friends?" I asked.

"No. Matthew studies History. I thought that he and Isla would make a cute couple, but Matthew told me that she's a, well, lesbian."

"Really?"

"Yes, but I'm quite forward thinking about these sorts of things. Richard doesn't know of course. I'm not sure how he would feel about it."

"Oh, does Richard not approve of gays and lesbians?"

Eleanor frowned. "Unfortunately not. This is a conservative town, as you know. Richard is against gay marriage."

"I'm not sure how well he'd do in Toronto then."

"Yes, well, Richard knows how to turn on his charm in public."

"Does he ever rant about his stance against gay marriage in this house?" I asked.

Eleanor thought about it and she turned even pinker with embarrassment. "Maybe. I hope he didn't offend Isla. She's really good with the kids and they adore her."

"What about Joanne and her husband? I haven't met her husband yet."

"They're lovely too. Henry does odd jobs around the house and works in the garden. He's a sweetheart. They'd been living in the house before we even moved in here. I guess you could say that they came with the place. They have their own section, adjacent to the garage. This house is very old and it has servants' quarters. But the good thing about their room is that they have their privacy."

"And you think they always enjoy working for your family?"

"I think so," Eleanor said. "They're lovely to me and the children, but I guess Richard can be a bit gruff and demanding. But he works so much and he's out of the house most of the time that they don't mind. I'd call them my friends."

"Are they well paid?" I asked.

Eleanor gave me an incredulous look. "I sure hope so. Sure Richard got his assistant to order them some thoughtless presents for Christmas. He gave Joanne a new vacuum and Henry a new rake. Richard thought it was funny, but I felt like the gifts were insulting, so I baked them cookies and got them gift certificates to go shopping at the mall."

"And your son – he's the son you had with your first husband, right?"

"Yes. He's all grown. Time goes by so fast. Can you believe it? His father lives in Calgary and Matthew is close to him. Luckily he likes the school he's in here so he's closer to me. Otherwise he'd be in Calgary and I'd never see him."

"Why? Does he not get along with his stepfather?"

"They get along okay. Don't speak much, but it's all right."

"I'm starting to get the picture that not a lot of people get along with your husband."

Eleanor laughed that same bitter laugh. "Yes. Well, he's not the easiest person to get along with. But he's powerful and he's got charisma, which was what attracted me to him in the first place, I suppose."

Speaking of the devil, Richard Champ's voice boomed from downstairs.

"Eleanor? Eleanor! Where are you?"

I jumped up and opened the door to the library and stuck my head out to the staircase.

Mayor Richard Champ was stomping up the stairs right at me.

Chapter 6

J oanne followed Richard Champ up the stairs, lecturing him for stomping on the carpet that she had just cleaned. Richard ignored her and kept calling Eleanor's name. He was waving a piece of paper around. His round face was flushed red and he was panting from running. When he saw me, he stopped and took a deep breath.

"Emma, hello."

"Is everything okay?" I asked.

"Where's Eleanor?"

"Right here." Eleanor appeared looking frightened. "What is it?"

"The bastards!" Richard waved the paper around. "Found this at my office."

He showed us the note.

Place $50,000 in a brown bag inside the mailbox in front of the Canoe Creek today at 6pm. The big one will take it. Any interference and the little one's gonna get it.

The ransom note was a lot less poetic this time. The Canoe Creek was a canoe rental place just outside of town near the lake. It was closed at this time of the year so the canoes were strapped and locked in and the place was more or less abandoned.

"I knew they wanted money," said Richard.

"What are we going to do?" Eleanor said.

"I already called the police. Once I get my hands on this guy, I'm sure he'll live to regret it. Just wait!"

The mayor paced in the hallway with a murderous look in his eyes. The police were on their way, which meant that Sterling, Sandra, or both, might show up. I dreaded the thought of meeting Sandra again so soon.

The news of the ransom note threw off my theory that the kidnapper was out for personal revenge. This was a disappointment, but I still had to keep up the investigation on my end to cover what Sandra wanted to ignore.

The note had been delivered. There was no handwriting this time; the writing was printed from a computer. The police would want to analyze the paper, the font, and the type of printer used to print it.

And what would I do? The only thing I could do – talk to the other people in the house. I went downstairs to find Joanne. As unpleasant as she was, I had to talk to her. When I got into the living room, I looked through the glass windows and saw the gardener shovelling snow in the backyard. It must've been Henry, Joanne's husband.

Could he have been the man I saw talking to the kids that day at the festival?

I stepped outside the glass windows to talk to him.

"Hello," I said. "I'm Emma, Eleanor's friend."

The man looked up at me and smiled. He was missing one of his front teeth, and his pale skin was as dry and wrinkly as his wife's, but his eyes were hazel and kind.

I made small talk. "It's cold outside today, huh?"

"Sure," he said. "But I'm not looking forward to this ice storm this weekend. I think I'll stay in then."

He chuckled. It was odd that he was in such good humour when his employers' children were missing.

"Yes," I said. "I hope those children are all right, wherever they are."

The smile remained on his face. "Little Zoe and Joseph, yes."

Henry didn't look too concerned that the children had been kidnapped. I thought they were supposed to be close.

"I have faith that they'll be back," Henry said, still smiling. "That's why I'm continuing my work, preparing the backyard for them to play in. Sure was a heavy snowfall yesterday."

"I suppose that's an optimistic way of looking at it," I said. "But aren't you concerned that maybe they are in real danger?"

The smile stayed on Henry's face. I was beginning to think that he was a bit out of it.

"If they are, what can we do? Worrying will only make it worse. The most that I can do is imagine that they're safe and sound and back here."

I thought that there *was* something that we could do: find out who did it. Henry and I must've had very different life philosophies.

"Any idea who would do such a thing?" I asked innocently.

He shook his head. "Beats me. But I'd rather not focus on this. I want to focus on the image that they're safe and sound."

"Yes." From the way his face looked with his permanent grin, I was starting to think that there was something mentally wrong with him. Still, I pressed on with my questions.

"How do you like working for the mayor? Must be a privilege, huh?"

"He's a bright man. He gets the work done in this town."

"What about at home? Is he a good father?"

Henry hesitated. I thought I saw his eyes dim. "The kids are lucky to have so many people working in the house and looking after them."

I nodded. This wasn't getting anywhere. Henry wasn't forthcoming with information. I had to go in another direction.

"When was the last time you saw the children?" I asked.

"Before they went to the Snowman Festival yesterday. Joanne was helping them with their hats and mittens."

"So the babysitter wasn't here to help?"

"Isla doesn't work on Sundays."

"I see. So you didn't go to the Snowman Festival?"

"Me? No. Had to paint the garage. Mr. Champ also wanted the toolshed to be cleaned."

"Wow, he works you hard, huh? Even during the festival, when you could be having fun?"

Henry shrugged. "Well, it's not an official holiday. Plus the festival's really for young people anyway. Working's good for an old man like me. Keeps the spirit young."

"So your wife didn't go either?"

"Oh no. Joanne, she doesn't like big crowds."

Henry was piling the snow up high and I didn't know what else to ask. All I knew was that they were both home when the others were out. Could they have done it? Henry seemed a bit slow, but could he have a crazy side stemming from his apparent mental illness?

When I went back inside, I heard yelling coming from upstairs.

I quickly snuck back up.

It was a male's voice that was shouting. An angry voice. It wasn't the mayor's because it wasn't as deep. I listened.

"Oh, so now that they're asking for money, you care?"

The door to the library was open, but I couldn't risk looking in without being seen.

"What are you implying?" the mayor bellowed.

"I don't think you give two shits about your kids," said the man. "You're more upset now that they're asking for your campaign funds. You weren't this upset when they were merely going to be murdered."

"Stop it, Matthew!" Eleanor cried. "Of course Richard cares about the children. He's just doing the best he can."

Eleanor was sobbing. It must've been her first son doing all the yelling.

"No, you stop, Mom. I don't know why you're defending him and making all these excuses for him when you *know* what he's like. Everybody knows. Hell, I know that you don't love each other, so why are you even here, Mom? So you can have all this? Well, the kids are gone. What are you going to do now?"

"Matthew, I know you're upset. Everybody is, but we have to pull together. The police are doing all they can. We have to keep together."

Matthew only stomped his feet and stormed out. I scurried behind the door so that he didn't see me. I listened to him charge down the stairs and slam the front door shut.

When I slipped out of the crack between the wall and the opened door, I rounded the corner and ran into Joanne at the bottom of the staircase. I almost gasped at the sight of her staring back at me with her narrowed eyes.

Chapter 7

"Are you still here?" she asked.

"Yes," I said. Blood rose to my cheeks from getting caught. I had to get better at my spying skills. "I was just going to say goodbye to Eleanor, but seeing as there's all this commotion..."

"You're not a reporter, are you?"

"No, no, of course not. I'm a musician."

She gave me a once-over. "Musician? What kind of music?"

"I sing. My style of music is contemporary blues and soul."

"I don't listen to music," she said.

"Right."

Who didn't listen to music?

"Got those journalists snooping around here all day yesterday, with their cameras and tape recorders. I had to shoo them away with my broom. Now the police are coming, wanting their coffee and donuts."

"Er, yes. They can be quite a nuisance. When are they coming exactly?"

"Any minute now."

I'd better question her fast if I wanted to get out before Sandra showed up.

"So that was some commotion now, with Matthew. Do they argue like this often?"

Joanne looked at me, then nodded. I could tell she wanted someone to vent to about the goings-on of the house. Now that I'd spoken to Henry, I figured that she had no one else to talk to about this sort of thing.

"Yeah, well, don't mind him, them two men never got along in this house."

"It must be extra upsetting for Matthew to have his siblings go missing. But why would he accuse the mayor of not caring?

"I don't blame Matthew really. Richard's always berating everyone around him. The kids, his wife, even us. Poor Henry. He must've called Henry a retard about a million times. Can you believe that?"

"That's terrible."

"He even calls me a lazy cow when I don't have the food ready on time."

"How do you stand it?" I asked.

"I don't know," she said grimly. "He attacks Henry of being mentally ill, but you know who's really ill? The mayor. He has two different personalities. To the public he's charming, loveable, all jokes and all smiles. If we're lucky, he's like that here when he's had a good day at work. But when he's cross, watch out. Luckily he works a lot. Ignores his kids really. Only uses them to pose for photo ops. Like at the Snowman Festival."

"Oh, were you there?"

"Yes," she said. "I mean, only passing by on my way home from the grocery store. I saw the kids on stage when the mayor was making a speech."

"I see. Well, who do you suspect kidnapped the kids?"

"Who knows?" she said. "Maybe it's those friends that he goes drinking with. Maybe he shows his true colors to them. I don't know where he goes with them. The wife doesn't ask."

"It must be such negative work environment here."

"Everybody else is nice," she said. "We all get along. Just the mayor is the bad egg. I suppose it's because he's a politician. After blood and power. They're all the same."

"What about the babysitter, Isla? How does she like working here?"

"Seems like a nice girl," she said. "Likes the kids. Doesn't like the mayor either, although she doesn't interact with him as much as we have to."

"So she's not coming in today, is she?"

"Why would she? The kids are gone. She's out of a job if they come back. God help them. Isla needs the work too."

"Why? Is she in financial trouble?"

"All I know is her father's unemployed and she's been working hard. And the mayor stiffed her on her Christmas bonus this year. University aint cheap and I think she's deep in student loans."

Before I could inquire further, the doorbell rang.

"Oh, they're here. Ate all the donuts last time, so none for them today."

Joanne bustled out to get the door.

I followed, wondering if I could slip out the back. Before I could even budge, Joanne threw the door open.

"What are you doing here?" Sandra asked, her dark eyes burning into mine.

Chapter 8

S terling stepped in behind her, along with two other policemen. Did they really need that many policemen to look at a note?

"Hi." I flashed my biggest smile to deflect Sandra's scowl. She didn't smile back.

"Hi, Emma." Sterling wore an amused expression. "I guess I shouldn't be surprised to see you here."

"Didn't I warn you about getting mixed up with official police business?" Sandra asked bluntly.

"I'm here to see Eleanor," I said innocently. "She's my friend. Is it a crime to visit a friend?"

Richard and Eleanor came down the stairs to greet the police. Richard's face was still red with anger, and Eleanor looked like she had been crying again.

I told Eleanor that I'd give them their privacy and would be going now. I could feel Sandra's eyes burning a hole into me as I walked past her.

When I went out the door, Sterling came out after me.

"Emma, wait."

He closed the door and grabbed my wrist.

"I'm sorry about my partner," he said.

"Yeah, well, it's not your fault, I guess."

"Everyone's on edge because of the case."

"I get it."

"I apologize for any rudeness on her part."

"You can't apologize for someone else, but I appreciate it. Any progress on the case?"

He shook his head, but I couldn't tell if it was because he didn't make any progress or if he just didn't want to tell me.

"That's okay if you can't tell me," I said. "How's your new partner working out anyway?"

"She's efficient. Of course I'd much rather be working with you. She is a bit hot tempered, so sometimes it helps with the suspects. I get to be the good cop for once, if you can believe it."

"I believe it." I smiled.

Sterling smiled back, but his expression dropped into an even more serious one. He put his hands on my shoulders.

"Listen, Emma, I know you like to do detective work, but this is a serious case. The people we are investigating are criminals. I don't want you snooping around and getting mixed up with something dangerous on your own, okay?"

"But Sterling —"

"Please." Sterling looked deeply into my eyes.

I looked back into Sterling's warm grey eyes. I wished he would put his strong arms around me to hug me and kiss me. I was tempted to initiate it, but this wasn't the time.

"I'm not getting mixed up with those guys," I said. "Don't worry."

It was the truth. I wasn't investigating other politicians and con artists. I was looking more into babysitters and housekeepers. But it would've sounded too silly to tell him. I would've if I'd had more proof.

I could've been completely off track as well.

Still, I wished I could work with Sterling like old times. Must that Sandra be around all the time?

"Let's talk when this is all over," Sterling said.

His look let me know that he was ready to hear my answer: whether I was choosing Nick or him.

"Okay." I smiled and he smiled back. I wondered if he could tell that I'd already chosen him.

I stood still, hoping that Sterling would lean in and kiss me. He only looked at my lips, considering it. I felt heat all over my body from his intense gaze.

"Sterling?" Sandra stuck her head out.

She blinked at us.

"So talk later?" Sterling said.

"Sure. Good luck with the case."

I watched Sterling walk back inside.

I knew I shouldn't take Sandra's nasty attitude so personally, but I couldn't help but wonder if this was the way things were going to be. Why did she find me to be such a nuisance? Maybe she had a little crush on Sterling. I saw the way she looked at him just now, as if he was her possession. And were they in fact on a date when I saw them at my ceremony, or was that just Sterling being nice and showing her around the town because she was new?

Maybe she was simply a hot-tempered cop. I didn't like the fact that Sterling made excuses for her behavior, but he was a gracious guy. He wouldn't slag her off behind her back, and I didn't expect him to.

As much as I ached to be with him, everybody was so worked up about the case and so was I. I just needed a bit more confidence in my own skills.

So far it sounded like everyone could be a suspect. Joanne obviously had issues with the family, but as a kidnapper, she wouldn't be spilling all her grievances on me, would she? Henry had mental issues, but was he crazy? Was his overly optimistic attitude a facade for a nasty dark side? Matthew sounded like he hated the mayor and resented his mother. Could he have kidnapped the kids to get back at them somehow? He was certainly angry. And what about Isla? Not accepted for being a lesbian in the Champ house, and full of financial burden, she had plenty of motive to make some quick cash as well.

As I thought about this, Mirabelle called me.

"So, part of the note sounded familiar," she said. "And I couldn't figure out why. Then I finally realized that it's from a Harold Winken poem. It's not very famous, but Winken was a local poet. Well, he grew up in Hartfield in the 1940s anyway. Then he traveled, had a sort of tramp lifestyle."

"Never heard of him," I said. "What is the poem?"

"All his poems are untitled, so they take the first line from each poem. This one's called 'At the Wake of Dusk, A Swallow called'. I found it in our library. It's actually an old book of mom's."

"Are you still at mom's house?" I asked.

"No, I went back to my house, but I have the book with me, so come over."

"Great, I'm waving down a cab, so I'll see you in five minutes."

When I got to Mirabelle's house, we dissected the poem.

"I think this poem is saying that life is transient and that we should love each other unconditionally," I said.

"Weird for someone who is threatening to kill little kids."

"Whoever it is is well read," I said.

"A poetry lover."

Something struck me. "Their babysitter is studying English Lit. Plus she had a day off when the kids were kidnapped."

"What, you think she's holding them ransom for tuition money or something?"

"Could be a possibility. Can I use your computer?"

"Sure," Mirabelle passed me her laptop on the coffee table.

"Let's see. *Isla Waterstone.*"

I typed the baby-sitter's name in Google to see what would pop up. The first two were links to another Isla Waterstone, an amateur figure skater from Iowa. The third link was the nanny. It was her profile page from Callen University's website. She was the secretary of C.U.' S Charity Association. Under her bio, it said that she loved road trips, video games and poetry slams. No picture.

"Well it is someone who knows their poetry," said Mirabelle. "But does that make her a kidnapper?"

"I'll have to find out. I wonder where she is now. I want to talk to her. Chances are she's in class. But who would know which class?"

I searched Isla on Facebook. I found her out of a dozen of other Isla Waterstones when I saw the name of her school in connection with one profile. Isla's profile picture was of the back of her head. She was standing over the lake. She had short brown hair, and seemed to be dressed very boyishly in a white hoodie and black leather jacket.

If I'd only seen her from the back this way in real life, I would've assumed that she was a guy. Perhaps she had been the "man" I saw at the festival?

She kept a huge portion of her profile private, but I was able to learn some basic facts about her.

She was in a relationship with a girl named Camille Frankfurt.

I went to Camille Frankfurt's page. Her profile was a lot more active. She was a trainer at the Hartfield Community Centre gym and her posts were mostly fitness tips, inspirational quotes and nutrition advice. Under her musical likes, my fan page was there.

"Look at you," Mirabelle said. "You have two million fans? That number's doubled since the last time I checked."

I chuckled. "I know; I'm popular."

"So she's a fan of yours. Are you going to to talk to her?

"Yes," I said. "Maybe she knows where Isla is right now."

"Here." Mirabelle gave me her keys. "Take my car."

"Thanks."

"Try not to get into too much trouble.

"I'll try," I said.

Chapter 9

I drove Mirabelle's adorable navy Mini Cooper to the community centre. The parking lot was full, probably because of all the seniors who enjoyed swimming during the day.

A middle-aged receptionist with hair like a beehive sat at the front desk. She smiled at me when I came in.

"Hello," I said. "I was wondering if I could see Camille Frankfurt?"

"Do you have a membership?" she asked.

"No."

"I'm afraid you need a membership for access to the gym."

"Oh, I don't need access. I'm not here to work out. I just wanted to talk to her."

"In that case, she is in the gym training someone at the moment. I don't know when she has a break, so you can go right on in and ask her."

"Thanks."

I used to go to the centre a lot as a child. Swimming was my favorite activity. I probably never even stepped into the gym more than twice growing up. Even now, I'd do yoga, Pilates and Zumba – anything other than being in a gym with all those sweaty machines. I just hated the smell of human sweat and mechanical machinery. Now that I was a celebrity, however, there was no avoiding gyms, or trainers, for too long, and I had to face the unpleasant odors more times than I could bear on some weeks when I had to be especially fit for a photo shoot or something.

The dreaded smell hit me when I walked past the pool and went into the gym portion of the building. There was also a squash court and a basketball court at the centre.

As I expected, the gym contained mostly retired seniors. I spotted Camille helping a man who appeared to be an octogenarian with leg lifts. Camille looked just like her profile picture except that a red headband held her blond hair away from her face and she wore red track pants to match. At the sight of her, I knew why she looked so familiar. I had shaken hands with her during Emma Wild Day.

When she saw me, her jaw dropped. She had been holding up the old man's leg, and she dropped it as she stood up and jumped in excitement. I cringed, hoping that a bone didn't crack.

"Emma Wild?" Camille squealed.

"Hi, Camille."

"Wow, I can't believe you know who I am."

"Of course," I said. "I remember meeting you at the meet and greet."

"There must've been hundreds of people there."

"Well, I did look you up before I came," I admitted.

"Are you here to work out?"

"I'm here to talk to you actually. If you have a moment."

"Me?" She abruptly turned to her client. "Let's take five, Bernie."

Bernie panted and stayed on the ground. With a weak arm, he felt the ground for his bottle of water.

"Is there a place more private where we can talk?" I asked.

"Sure. We can go to the squash court. It's hardly ever booked at this time of day."

We left the gym, and left Bernie to his well-de-served break.

There were no seats in the squash court and we had to stand. Camille was still looking at me the way fans looked at celebrities – not quite believing that we were made of flesh and bones.

"I thought you were out of town," she said. "I read that you were going to start promoting your third album. I can't wait for its release, by the way!"

"Thanks. I'll be sure to send you a signed copy."

"Really? That would be so great. You're really the nicest."

"No problem. I'm sorry to cut into your time at work. I just wanted to ask whether you knew Isla Waterstone."

Camille face dropped. "Oh. Isla? Sure, she's my girlfriend. At least, I thought she was. I'm not sure how we stand right now. She hasn't been returning my calls lately."

I frowned. "You mean you're broken up?"

"I don't know. That's the weird part. We used to talk all the time, and I tried to reach out to her when I found out that the kids she was babysitting were kidnapped, but she seems to be avoiding me. Why? Are you looking for her too?"

I nodded. "I'm a friend of Eleanor Champ's. I wanted to talk to Isla to see if she knew anything to help with the case."

"I wish I could tell you. I even went around to her dad's house yesterday, but he was so drunk and didn't seem to know his own whereabouts, never mind hers."

"Does she do this often? Disappear and flake out every so often?"

"No, I don't think so," said Camille. "Well, we've only been dating for six months, but I thought we had a serious thing going on, you know? I mean, I hope she's alive. Unless she broke up with me and didn't want to break the news to me. In that case, I don't care if she's alive or not."

"Strange," I said.

"I think she's just avoiding me. If she wanted to break up, she should just do so. I hate it when people are dishonest. But I should've seen it coming. She'd been acting weird for a couple of weeks before. She'd be taking calls during our dates and would leave to go to the other room. When she came back, she'd act all weird when I'd ask who she was talking to."

"How many times has this happened?"

"Well, three times. I remember that the last time was when she was waiting out the front of the community centre when I was getting off work. She had been on the phone and got off in a hurry, saying something about helping a classmate. But she's not the best liar. She blinks a lot when she lies. And she seemed distracted. I thought it was because the holidays were over and she was readjusting back to her school schedule, but I don't know."

"That's really odd," I said. "Would she be in school right now?"

"I think so," she said. "I swear, if I find out she's been cheating on me..."

Camille took a deep breath.

"What class would she have right now?" I asked.

"I think she has Modern Poetry. It ends at four. At the Peterson Building."

"Oh, speaking of poetry, does she like Harold Winken by any chance?"

"Like it?" Camille laughed. "The girl is obsessed with Winken."

Chapter 10

As I drove the Mini Cooper out of Hartfield to Callen University, which was about thirty minutes away, I went over all I knew about Isla Waterstone.

She was definitely secretive online. There were no face shots of her online, not even in Camille's albums. Camille had explained that Isla hated having her photo taken and would block out her face with her arm if a camera so much as came near her.

She apparently loved the kids, but she was in debt. Plus she hated the mayor and had been acting strange and M.I.A. with Camille. And the Harold Winken obsession? It was not looking good for our girl Isla.

I called Eleanor.

"Do you happen to have a picture of Isla?" I asked.

"Sure, I have some pictures of her with the kids. Why do you need them?"

"I'm just curious to know what she looks like."

"Okay," she agreed. "Whatever I can do to help. I just really hope it's not her, because she's a sweet girl."

"If you can send me a photo as soon as possible, that would be great."

"If I can find it on my phone, I can forward one to you right away."

"Thanks," I said. "How is everything going? Did the police find anything yet?"

"Well, they are still looking for this old enemy of Richard's, but I don't know. We haven't heard anything back yet."

"That's too bad."

"Do you really think Isla is a suspect?"

"We'll see," I said vaguely. "But isn't it odd that she hasn't been around since the kidnapping, not even to comfort you?"

"Odd? Well, now that you mention it. I suppose, but I assumed she was busy with school. I've been so worried that I haven't thought about Isla not being around. You're right; it would've been nice if she called. I thought we were close."

"Hmm, well. Did you know that she's a big fan of Harold Winken?"

"Oh, the poet? Yes. She's a huge fan. She was always quoting him to us, so much so that I started reading Winken. Matthew and Joanne have taken to his poetry too, and I didn't think they were the poetry type. Even Henry has been quoting Winken. We have all his poetry collections. The house is Winken mad."

"Really?"

Damn. There went my argument against Isla. But at least it did prove that it was someone close to the family.

"How many people outside of your family know that your household is crazy about Winken?"

"Plenty, I suppose. Why?"

"Are you aware that a portion of the first ransom note is from a Winken poem?"

"No. Really?"

"Yes." I recited the lines to her.

"Oh my God." Eleanor gasped. "I didn't know. I mean, we do have dinner guests here sometimes, so maybe there are people who do know. I really didn't think it could be my staff."

"Well, we don't know anything yet," I assured her. "However, I'm trying to find out more about Isla. When was the last time she came into work?"

"The day before the Snowman Festival."

"Did she act unusual at all?"

"No. Well, she was a bit stressed, but she was talking about a project she was working on for school, so she had her reasons."

"Hmm, okay. Thanks."

I hung up. The only thing to do was to find her and talk to her. Why was she M.I.A. with her girlfriend? Was that really her way of breaking up with her girlfriend, or was she merely busy with school? Or could there have been some other explanation – like planning a big kidnapping plot against the employer she hated so she could pay off her student debts?

I pulled up to the school. Now that people were aware of who I was in this town, staying incognito was a luxury. But I really wanted to be a good spy. Usually my bright red hair was a dead giveaway so it was tied back into a bun and covered with a black beanie hat. I was dressed in my spying outfit of black pants and a black turtleneck sweater. My face was completely bare, so pale that I looked like a snowman myself. You wouldn't believe how much hair and makeup could transform a girl. Given enough of a makeup artist's magic, I had the theory that most women could look like celebrities. That was why I tried not to take the title too seriously. Like anything, it came with perks and downsides.

Eleanor sent me a picture with a clear shot of Isla's face. She was with the kids. They had built a castle out of foam blocks in the living room and Isla was kneeling between the two of them, smiling.

I pulled up to the building that Camille mentioned and checked the time. I was early because sometimes class let out early. At least that was what people who had gone to university have told me. I'd never gone to college, forgoing school in favor of a music career. I didn't regret it for the most part, although seeing all the college students walking around with their books and chatting together in groups made me long for the experience.

Not that I was ever a huge fan of being in school. I hated high school. But I admit I did have a chip on my shoulder for missing college, because it was the experience most people had. I'd missed the fun parties and clubs. And friends my age who were normal. Even sitting in a lecture would've been fun once in a while. Maybe.

Now that I was there, I did like the feel of a campus. The buildings were brown and old. I bet it smelled old too. It was quite a contrast to sleek hotels and big stadiums. Or the hole-in-the-wall bars where I sang when I was first starting my music career.

Maybe some part of me did want go to university even when I was young – maybe it wasn't about following Sterling as I'd always believed. Part of it was probably that I did long for the normal experience that others got to have. Although the other part of me, the part who wanted to sing and be on stage, was a lot louder. So loud that I listened and followed it. Then I actually got what I wanted. My career exploded. I couldn't regret my decision, right? How many other girls were struggling to be singers? I struggled and I made it. That was something to be proud of. I knew that after awhile I would've gotten tired of the campus life and would've been aching to go out and sing.

After waiting for another ten minutes in the car, students began streaming out the front doors. I watched for the face in Eleanor's photograph.

In the photo, Isla was dressed in a black T-shirt, jeans, and black Converse sneakers. She had a short boyish haircut, a round face, and a thin but fit frame. What if I missed her if she was wearing a hat or a hood or something? I tried to carefully look at each face, but it was a strain, sitting in that car, to try to look at everyone. And I was also trying not to look too eager.

The students weren't too quick to move because the weather was nice today. The air was still and the snow was fresh and crunchy on the ground – not too much slush yet, except in the gutters. The students stood in circles, chatting away, and many smoked and tried to look cool.

It made me think of Nick. Nick used to smoke, right around the time I met him. On our second date I told him that I didn't like men who smoked, but on the third time we went out, he showed me his patch and told me that he vowed to quit. And he did. It was hard when he had to do a film when he had to smoke, but he used herbal cigarettes.

It was sweet how he quit for me. I did love him, but I couldn't be with both Nick and Sterling. Of course, Nick wouldn't be single for long. Girls were always buzzing around him like bees to honey. Maybe that was part of the reason I chose Sterling too: the insecurity that I would lose Nick and that I was replaceable by the bevy of Hollywood girls who came onto the scene every day.

Finally Isla came out. She was wearing black jeans, the same black Converse sneakers, and a puffy navy winter jacket. She could've been mistaken for boy, although a very pretty one.

Isla walked towards one crowd of smokers and lit up. She smoked and chatted with them for a bit, laughing and in a good mood. I wanted to wait until she was alone to approach her in case I got recognized by a bunch of college kids, but the crowd lingered.

Then something interesting happened. A petite girl with long curly blond hair came up behind Isla. They separated from the crowd and kissed. They were all over each other in front of that school.

Camille was right. Isla was cheating on her. Or dumped her. But it did seem like she had a thing for blondes.

They began walking, and I didn't know whether to drive on, or get out and follow them. It didn't matter because Isla stopped in the middle of the sidewalk and answered the phone. She signalled to the blond girl that it was a private call and that she had to go. She quickly kissed her goodbye and turned the corner. I quickly restarted the car and followed her around the corner.

I pulled up to the curb and waited to see what she would do next. I couldn't decide whether to get out, follow her and try to listen in on the conversation, or to continue to tail her in my car. I was more comfortable in my car. There were way too many people around to stay incognito for long.

I didn't have to decide because Isla took out her keys and unlocked her Jeep. The old Jeep was black and looked like it was from the 80s. Where did Isla have to go that was so important? Although one little mystery was solved – whether she was cheating on Camille or not – there were plenty of other reasons why I still suspected her.

So I followed her. I made sure to stay two to three cars behind her so that she wouldn't catch me. Whenever I was in L.A. and driving around, I could always tell who was tailing me. The paparazzi, however, didn't know a thing about being inconspicuous.

She drove off, back in the direction of Hartfield.

I was disappointed when she pulled into the parking lot of a supermarket. This was her important errand? Maybe she wasn't the kidnapper; maybe she was just a normal college girl after all. I could still go in and ask her questions, but I didn't want her to know that I'd been following her. She was probably going home so I figured that I'd wait and follow her to her house. If she had anything suspicious going on at her house, I'd be more apt to find out. What if her father was in on it? He didn't exactly sound like a first-class citizen. Anything was possible.

Sterling had told me that this was what detective work was like sometimes, all the waiting around in cars. Frankly, it wasn't that exciting. Nick played a spy in his action movie, *Alive or Dead*. That looked a lot more exciting. Spying was only fun in the movies. Plus, Nick had been super sexy in that role.

The sun set while I waited. It sure got dark fast in January. I was beginning to feel sleepy.

Isla finally came out with three plastic bags of groceries. She placed them in the back of the car and then drove off.

As I drove after her, my phone rang. It was Sterling.

"Emma, hey."

"What's up?"

"What are you up to?" he asked casually, or trying to sound casual.

"I'm just grocery shopping," I said.

"You? Grocery shopping? Shouldn't you have an assistant for that?"

"No. But in New York, my housekeeper did it."

"Okay, well, I know that you know about the new ransom note," he said.

"The one about the money?" I asked.

"Yes. And I just have this feeling that you are going to get involved somehow."

I hadn't planned out what to do yet, but he was right: I was planning on going to the Canoe Creek later, but I had been hoping that I would figure out who did it before it came to that so there wouldn't need to be a big showdown.

"What do you mean?" I asked innocently.

"You know what I mean. I just wanted to warn you because we've got a lot of undercover guys covering the whole thing. We have the Canoe Creek bugged and everything. There'll be guns. It'll be too dangerous for you."

"Guns? But you know the kidnapper will be with the kids."

"We're going to be careful, but if this guy is armed, it's a possibility. That's just a worst-case scenario, but I don't want you to be in a dangerous situation like that. The guns are just for protection, and we might not use them, especially if the kids are involved, but if this guy is armed and dangerous, we are prepared. And I think we figured out part of his plan. We discovered that there's a hidden section in the Canoe Creek after talking to a historian about the place. There used to be a hidden speakeasy in the basement and there's a passage out that leads to the forest. So I think this guy will use this tunnel tonight."

"Really? Wow. That's crazy."

"Yes. So we're stationed around the area in the forest where the tunnel leads to."

"Just tread lightly," I said. "Remember those kids."

"Promise me that you won't get involved. We have plenty of men on this case. Please promise me."

I couldn't do that.

"Sterling, I think we're breaking up. Can't hear you."

"Emma..."

I hung up.

Isla's Jeep was still in my sight, but we weren't in Hartfield. We were going further out north, into the woods. Isla lived in Hartfield. Where would she go?

As we made our way farther up and the cars became scarce on the road, I turned my headlights off. As long as I stayed close enough to Isla, I could still see enough of the road.

She kept going, driving right up into the woods. I'd been up to this neck of the woods once. My high school friend Jennifer's family had a cabin up here, and I used to come here with her on some weekends.

What was Isla doing near these cabins?

She pulled up to a moderately sized cabin. We were surrounded by trees. The moon was out and it was a spooky place to be. I parked a good distance away from her. Thankfully Mirabelle's car was dark and blended in. There was no time to hide the car. Isla was moving fast.

I got out and followed her. Each step crunched the snow. It sounded extra loud in the silence.

She approached the cabin and I saw Isla drop the bag of groceries on the porch and walk away. Then she pulled out her phone and began texting. This was odd. I got closer, and Isla walked away, back into her car and I heard her drive off.

I prayed that she didn't see my car on her way out.

When she was gone, I waited. There were shadows moving in the light of the cabin windows.

The most bizarre sight greeted me when the door of the cabin opened. I gasped.

Chapter 11

It was one of the costumes from the Snowman Festival. There had been at least six of those guys running around at the festival. But this snowman was in a cabin in the middle of the night.

I also heard kids' voices. Could they be the mayor's kids? When the door closed, I inched closer. The porch light seemed to be automatic, so I went to one of the side windows.

Slowly I inched up and peeked into one of them. It was Zoe and Joseph! They were jumping up and down because of the food. The snowman put a felt hand into the bag and got out some candies. The kids actually looked happy.

So this was where they were? Kidnapped by a crazy person dressed like a snowman? It could've been anyone.

Isla was involved, but was she the mastermind? She had dropped off the food, so she definitely knew what she was doing. The question was, who was in that snowman suit?

Maybe it was one of her friends and she was paying them off.

At least the kids weren't hurt in any way. I began to back away slowly. I took out my phone to tell Sterling where I was and what I found out.

But suddenly a face appeared before me.

I almost screamed.

"So you've been the one following me around. I knew I wasn't being paranoid."

Isla looked at me in the moonlight with one eyebrow raised.

I jumped back, arms up and ready to fight. It was the Krav Maga training.

"Wow, take it easy." Isla jumped back herself. "I don't want to fight. Who are you?"

"I'm a friend of Eleanor's."

Her eyes grew wide.

"Really?"

"You might want to tell me what you're doing with these kidnapped kids."

I talked a mean talk, but I was actually very scared. What if Isla had a gun? She did kidnap these kids after all.

"I know it looks bad, but…"

She stuttered, nervous, and I realized that I had the upper hand.

"Keep talking or I'll call the police," I said roughly.

"Okay, okay. I was just helping. I didn't actually kidnap the kids. I found out about it, and I was talked into helping. I mean, it was for the mayor's own good. He treats his children like shit. He treats everyone like shit. But I didn't know it was going to go this far, with the money and everything. I just wanted to make sure that the kids were okay and well-taken care of."

"That's why you brought them the food?" I looked at her, still not completely trusting the story. "How much are you getting out of this?"

"I don't know," she said. "Like I said, I didn't know that there would be money involved. It wasn't even my plan."

"Then whose was it? Who's the guy in the suit?"

"Please don't tell the police," Isla begged. "God, it wasn't supposed to get this serious."

"How is kidnapping not serious?" I asked. "If you tell me, I'll try to help you, but the police are on your trail. They will find out."

Her eyes got even wider. "No, please don't. I'm on a scholarship. I can't be a criminal." Isla began to cry. "I can't deal with any more pressure these days."

"Do you have any idea how serious this is? There are dozens of armed policemen ready to take the kidnapper down. We have to put a stop to this."

"Okay, okay I'll tell you."

She let out a big sigh.

When Isla told me the name of the kidnapper, I wasn't completely surprised. Why hadn't I realized it sooner? Of course. No wonder the snowman suit was required.

"I really didn't think it would go this far," Isla said. "As far as I knew, it was supposed to be a prank to retaliate against the mayor."

"Yes, but Eleanor is in absolute panic."

"I just feel awful. Of course she would be. It's so stupid of me. I just wanted to make sure the kids were okay."

"Don't worry," I said, "Now just go tell your snowman to call the thing off."

When we headed back to the house, we noticed all the lights were off. We heard an engine start. A car was driving away!

"Oh no!" Isla cried. "They've gone to the Canoe Creek."

"I didn't know there was another car."

"It's rented," said Isla. "Just for the occasion. It was parked on the other side of the house."

"I see," I said. "Let's go stop them. Otherwise, you'll be in big trouble. I'll take the kids to the police and I won't mention your name if I can avoid it. If you'll just help me now."

Isla nodded.

"Come on," I said. "Let's drive."

She got into the passenger side of my car.

"Tell me the best way to go to Canoe Creek," I said.

She gave me the directions and told me what the plan was.

"Zoe has been instructed to take the money from the mailbox at the Canoe Creek. Then she would go back into the Canoe Creek. There's a secret passage in there. There used to be a speakeasy in the basement, and there's a tunnel connected to the speakeasy from the forest in case the patrons needed to sneak out."

"And this little girl is going to do this? Wouldn't she be scared?"

"Well, Zoe is a tough little girl. She's very bright, and was taught what to do as a sort of game. She was supposed to be dropped off in the woods, get the money, go into the Canoe Creek, and head straight into the tunnel."

"You know what?" I said to her. "The police know about your plan. They're going to catch them right at the tunnel's entry in the forrest. And the men will be armed."

"Oh no." Isla exclaimed. "I'm so stupid for not talking them out of this. Now the kids are really in danger too."

I looked ahead in the darkness. "I don't see their car."

"Their headlights could be off." She sighed. "It could be too late. They could be there already."

Chapter 12

A s we continued to the Canoe Creek, I tried calling Sterling. He didn't answer and I had to leave a message telling him who the kidnapper was.

I was afraid that they would do something drastic to seriously hurt the kidnapper in the snowman suit.

When we drove up, the place looked dead. Not a sound. The police must've been hiding. The situation was beginning to scare me. I checked my watch. It was almost six.

I couldn't believe that the kidnapper would actually be driving in that snowman suit.

"I tried on the costume once," Isla said. "Just the head. You can actually see through the eye holes quite easily, and there are sound holes for the ears and around the neck, so it's not that bad."

"Still, it takes dedication. Let's just hope that your friend gets out of this unscathed. The mayor must've put the money in the box already."

Then we saw her. Zoe came out of the woods and ran to the mailbox. Gingerly, she stuck her hands into the box and pulled out a thick envelope. $50,000 in bills wasn't as much as you would think.

"Do you know where the end of the tunnel is?" I asked Isla.

"Yes," she said. "But, I wouldn't know how to get there by car because it's in the woods."

"Are they going back to the cabin after?"

"Yes."

Just then, we saw a couple of cops run into the Canoe Creek with guns in their holsters.

I looked at Isla accusingly. "I can't believe you guys would let the kids be in this situation. They're going to be scared to death."

"I know. I'm sorry. But what can we do?"

"Is the snowman armed?" I asked.

"I don't think so. Wait, maybe he is. They do keep a spare gun in the cabin."

"If they so much as catch a glimpse of a gun, what if they fire?"

Once we got into the woods, we became quiet. I was scared because I knew there were armed policemen all around us. Isla continued to lead the way.

We ran, and I tripped over a branch and fell on my knees.

"Oufff!"

"Are you okay?" Isla whispered.

"Fine." I grimaced.

We kept going, until we saw a glint of metal under the moonlight: the rented car. Then we saw the snowman, its face white underneath the moonlight. Joseph, the little boy, sat in the passenger seat.

"Just crazy," I muttered.

We approached and saw a shadow sprint before us.

"It must be a cop," I said. "They must've seen the car too."

"They're surrounding him."

"We gotta go stop them."

We ran to the car just as Zoe ran out of the tunnel and jumped into the car.

I saw a few of the men in the shadows, armed with guns.

Isla gasped. "Stop them!"

The snowman hugged the boy close.

One of the men was Sterling. I could tell by the way his hair fell in the back of his head, its specific swirl.

"Sterling!"

He looked back at me.

"Emma, what are you doing here? This is not the time."

"I know who the kidnapper is!"

"Who?"

"It's Matthew, Eleanor's son. He's not a dangerous criminal. Hold your fire."

Just then, the snowman drove off, but the police fired anyway, aiming at the tires so that the car sputtered and deflated.

"Oh my god." Isla cried at the sound of the gunfires.

"Stop!" Sterling cried to the men on his team.

Sandra appeared on the scene. She was in her pantsuit with a black coat over it.

Isla called out to the car, to Matthew. "They know it's you. Just give it up, move slowly and you'll be fine."

He did. It was a funny sight: a snowman coming out of the car. The men surrounded him and got him into handcuffs.

"Okay, but please don't take off this costume," Matthew said. "I don't want the kids to know that it's me."

I supposed he was like a person in character at Disneyland. Taking off the costume might've been traumatizing to the kids.

"This is absolutely ludicrous," Sandra said.

The police took Matthew away. The kids came out and hugged Isla.

"Where's the Snowman going?" Joseph asked. "He said we were playing a scavenger hunt."

"Is Matthew in trouble?" Zoe asked.

Isla frowned. "How did you know it was Matthew?"

Zoe rolled her eyes. "Of course I knew it was him. I'm not a baby you know. I also know that there's no such thing as Santa Claus either."

"Yes there is," Joseph insisted.

"No, Joseph. The presents are really from mom and dad. I told you already."

Tears formed in Joseph's eyes. "No, they're from Santa," he wailed.

Sterling turned to me. "How did you know that it was Matthew?"

"It's a long story," I said.

Sandra came back to our group. "Come on, let's go to the station. Tom, can you bring the children back to their parents?"

The officer on the scene nodded.

"Can I go with them?" Isla asked. "I want to explain my part in this to Eleanor."

"Just let her go," I said to Sandra and Sterling. "She helped me get here. She's not going anywhere."

Chapter 13

"**J**ust say it," Sterling said.

He was driving and Miss Pantsuit was sitting beside him. I was in the backseat, feeling like a criminal with these two cops up in front.

"Say what?" I asked innocently.

"I told you so."

I grinned. "But it would be too easy."

He sighed. "We should've listened to you, okay? We should've scooped out who was close to the family too. We did find out that the ink and printer from the second note was printed on the same type of printer that the Champ family owned, so we did start thinking like you then."

Sandra turned back and looked at me rather coldly. "How did you figure it out?"

"It was rather difficult," I said diplomatically. "There wasn't a lot to go on. All I knew was that I saw someone talking to the kids at the festival. I was sure it was a guy. Isla told me everything. It was actually Matthew, telling the kids to meet a snowman at the snow cone stand after they finish building their snowman. He was going to have surprise presents for them. So the kids hurried to finish up their snowman for the contest so they could get their gifts. By the time they did, Matthew was in his snowman costume."

I told him about having my suspicions towards Henry, Joanne and Isla, and ultimately decided that Isla had the strongest motives, so I followed her. Surprisingly, she led me to Matthew.

"But what was Matthew's motive?" Sterling asked.

"He never got along with the mayor. In fact he hated him, hated how he verbally abused the kids, his mom, and the staff."

"Did he physically abuse them?" Sterling asked with concern.

"Not as far as I know."

"Because we'd book him for that."

"Matthew just wanted some revenge. He wanted to see the mayor get worked up. Matthew didn't seem to be pleased with his mother either, because she'd stayed with him for superficial reasons. Since Isla hated the mayor too, Matthew managed to convince her to help him buy food and run errands so the kids were well taken care of in the cabin. Oh, and they'd been staying at a cabin by the way. It's actually the Champ family cabin. Matthew thought that because he was dressed like the snowman, the kids wouldn't recognize him."

"I'm sorry for not listening to you," said Sterling. He nudged Sandra.

She cleared her throat. "Yes. Good job, Wild."

Sterling nudged Sandra again. "And sorry for slamming a door in your face. I tend to do that under high stress situations."

"Apology accepted," I said. Although I was pretty certain Sandra still hated my guts and we wouldn't be BFFs any time soon.

"It's going to be a crazy night," Sterling said. "Lots of action at the police station. The mayor will be furious."

"But knowing the mayor," I said, "he probably wouldn't want word to spread that it was Matthew. He would want to keep his reputation of having a perfect family."

"Yes," Sterling said. "He'll probably spin it as a family joke gone wrong. Too bad it's not anytime close to April Fool's Day. Anyway, I'm sure he'll come up with some excuse to save face. Was Matthew after money as well?"

"I don't know. But when he saw that the mayor wasn't as affected by the ransom note as he'd hoped, he introduced the money element. That really got the mayor riled up."

Sterling shook his head. "Some people are just horrible."

"Big cities or small towns, political families are just the same anywhere, aren't they?" Sandra said.

We drove on for a while, out of the woods and back to Hartfield. I yawned. It had been a long day and I was starving. I'd barely eaten lunch. Being an amateur spy really took a toll on your body.

"I'll drop you home first," Sterling said.

"Great," I murmured before closing my eyes involuntarily.

By the time he pulled up to the Wild house, I was practically asleep. When Sterling opened the door on my side, my vision of him was blurred.

"I'm going to walk her up," he told Sandra.

I yawned and stretched in the back seat. Sterling looked at me as if I were an adorable kitten.

"Be quick," Sandra said. "Because we have to go to the station ASAP."

Sterling helped me out of the car. He held me by putting an arm around my shoulders as we walked up the stairs. I was still a bit groggy, but I exaggerated my sleepiness so that I could feel Sterling's arm around me. By the time we reached the top step of the porch, I felt like I'd melted into his arms.

In the month that we were apart, I had missed him terribly, and I hadn't wanted to admit to myself just how much I did.

I wanted to tell him that I chose him, but Sandra was in the car, glaring at us. Why was she concerned with our business? I really did think that she had a thing for Sterling.

To piss her off, I could've leaned in for that kiss, but it didn't feel right. A kiss had to be pure and full of love, not performed to spite someone.

"Have a good night then." Instead I gave Sterling my warmest smile and went inside.

Chapter 14

Early next morning, I went to Eleanor Champ's house again. We'd agreed to a brunch date. Joanne led me to the dining room to see her.

Eleanor's eyes were once again swollen when I came in.

She gave me a tight hug and I patted her back. When she pulled back, I could breathe again. She pointed to a chair.

"Please, sit."

I did, letting her compose herself a bit.

Brunch was already prepared – salmon quiche with Greek salad. A bottle of red wine was opened as well. Eleanor had already helped herself to a glass.

"How is everything?" I asked.

"I'm just glad that the kids are all right."

The kids could be heard running down the stairs and into the living room. Zoe was chasing Joseph around and Joseph was laughing with delight.

"Usually I'd tell them to quiet down, but I'm just so happy that they're safe that they can do whatever they want at this point."

"I'm glad," I said. "So how are Matthew and Richard handling all this?"

"Richard doesn't plan on pressing charges. He's furious as hell, but at least he's not doing anything to harm Matthew, as long as Matthew does community service hours for the next three months. And, well, Matthew decided to transfer schools to be with his father in Calgary as soon as the semester is over."

"I'm sorry to hear that."

Eleanor sighed. "I don't want him to leave. But better that he leaves than to end up in jail and get a criminal record that could ruin his life, right?"

"He did try to extract $50,000 from the town mayor," I said. "He's lucky that he got off easy."

"Yes," Eleanor said. "He's my son and I love him, but if it were up to me, I *would* put him in jail for a few days to teach him a lesson. He'd be scared half to death. What hurts is that he knew his actions would hurt me too. I know he's acting out, but this was just so extreme. He'd always been an intense kid, very sensitive, but I didn't raise him to be cruel."

"Maybe it's the mayor who can be blamed for that," I said. "So will your relationship change with Matthew?"

"Yes, but I also think my relationship will change the most with my husband. Matthew is right. I don't love Richard, and I'm not doing anybody any favors by being with him, least of all myself. I plan on getting a divorce in the coming months."

"Wow."

Eleanor sniffed. "Yes. I'm brave enough to do it this time."

She nodded, as if it was the fuel she needed to propel herself to believe it.

"Good for you," I said. "Why stay in a marriage if you're not happy?"

"Yes. It took me long enough to realize it. I always said I was staying for the kids, and to help Richard keep his image as a family man, but really, I'm scared. I'm scared not to have the security, scared of being divorced again, of being alone again."

I put a hand over her hand. She began to tear up again.

"Of course, I'll wait a bit. I want to make sure Matthew is safe from Richard's wrath. I'll divorce after the reelection. If he's reelected, great, if not, he doesn't need me anyway."

"You're strong," I said, looking her in the eyes.

She sniffed and laughed it off, embarrassed. "Thank you, Emma, for everything. I feel like such a fool, blubbering and crying around such a famous singer. But you're sweet. You're really a Hartfield girl. I'm proud that you're representing this town."

"No problem," I said.

She blew her nose into a tissue and then laughed.

"What happened to Isla?" I asked.

"She's fired. She was great, but it would've been unthinkable to keep her. Richard was tempted to press charges, but he wanted to hush her up as well. Poor girl. She has an unemployed, off-the-wagon father to take care of. I hope she finds a better job. I'd be happy to give her a recommendation, but if Richard ever gets wind of who she'll work for next, he'll want to talk to the family and destroy her in the little ways that he can."

"He's kind of scary, huh?"

Eleanor shrugged. "He's my husband."

Chapter 15

I was stuffed after brunch with Eleanor. At least things worked out in the end. No one was hurt, the kids were happy and healthy, and Eleanor seemed to be on track to living the life she wanted, even if she had to go through some obstacles first.

The first thing I did when I left her house was call Sterling. He didn't answer, but I left a message saying that I would be trying him at his office.

Now that this whole kidnapping fiasco was over, I had to face my own life – namely my love life. But I had it sorted out this time. I knew the man I wanted to spend the rest of my life with. He was my first love and I wanted him to be my last. I wondered if he had gotten any sleep last night. Either way, he could always benefit from a coffee or two. With me.

When I got to the station, the people working there looked at me in a new light. They had looks of admiration in their eyes, not unlike the fans I often met backstage at concerts.

"Good work, Miss Wild." An older officer approached me and shook my hand. "You saved everyone here a lot of grief."

"Thanks." I flashed a smile at everyone. "Good work yourselves, guys."

"Can I get an autograph?" A younger cop came up with a pad of paper. "My name is Steve."

"Sure, Steve." I wrote him a quick message and handed it back to him. He turned pink and grinned bashfully.

"I'm looking for Sterling. Is he in?"

"Yes," said the older officer. "In his office."

"Great."

I couldn't wait to see him. It was finally time.

When I got to his office I noticed that the curtains of the glass window were drawn closed. Even though they were never closed. I tried the door handle, but it was locked. I was about to knock when I noticed that there was a crack in the curtains and that I could peek through it. Something compelled me to look.

What I saw disturbed me. It was Sandra on top of Sterling in his chair. Her body was on his, pressing down on him hard. Her top was unbuttoned, showing ample cleavage.

I let out a gasp and felt a sinking feeling within me. Just when I was about to cry, anger took over and I pounded on the door.

Snow Cone Recipes

To make snow cones at home, you can buy a snow cone maker for under $20, or you can use a food processor to crush the ice.

Put the ice shavings in a cup or bowl. Now you can make different flavored syrups to drizzle and drench the ice.

Kool-Aid Snow Cones

- 1 cup water

- 2 cups granulated sugar

- 1 packaged Kool-Aid powder (any flavor)

Mix sugar and water in a saucepan and bring to a boil. Mixture should be clear. Stir in the drink mix until completely dissolved. Set aside to cool completely. Drizzle over shaved ice with a spoon or from a squirt bottle.

Raspberry-Blueberry Snow Cones

- 3 cups blueberries
- 2 1/2 cups raspberries
- 1/2 cup sugar
- 1/2 water
- 8 cups shaved ice

This is a more sophisticated snow cone recipe with real fruit and fruit juice.

Coarsely mash 2 cups blueberries and 1 1/2 cups raspberries with water and sugar in a saucepan with a potato masher. Boil uncovered for 3 minutes, stirring occasionally. Pour mixture to a blender and blend until almost smooth. Pour it through a sieve into a bowl, discarding solids. Cool syrup, then chill in fridge loosely covered in plastic wrap, for about 1 hour.

Serve 3 tablespoons of syrup over 1 cup of shaved ice. Top with 1/4 cup remaining mixed berries. Makes 8 servings.

Mango Strawberry Snow Cones

- Ice
- 2 mangoes, peeled and chopped
- 1 pint strawberries

A quick and easy dessert. Fill a food processor with ice and process until the ice is fine. Add mangoes and strawberries and pulse to blend together. Serve in a dessert glass or dish. Garnish with a lime wedge if you wish and serve immediately.

About the Author

Harper Lin lives in Kingston, Ontario with her husband, daughter, and Pomeranian puppy. When she's not reading or writing mysteries, she's in yoga class, hiking, or hanging out with her family and friends. She lived in Paris in her twenties, which inspired *The Patisserie Mysteries*.

She is currently working on more cozy mysteries.

www.HarperLin.com

www.ingramcontent.com/pod-product-compliance
Lightning Source LLC
Chambersburg PA
CBHW02195919062

46808CB00017B/2857